Spotty ball

Stripy ball

Beach ball

Tennis ball

Jingly ball

Golf ball

Dog ball

Woolly ball

Starry ball

Baseball

No ball

Squashed ball

Basketball

Book ball

SQUEAK

Squeaky ball

Spare ball

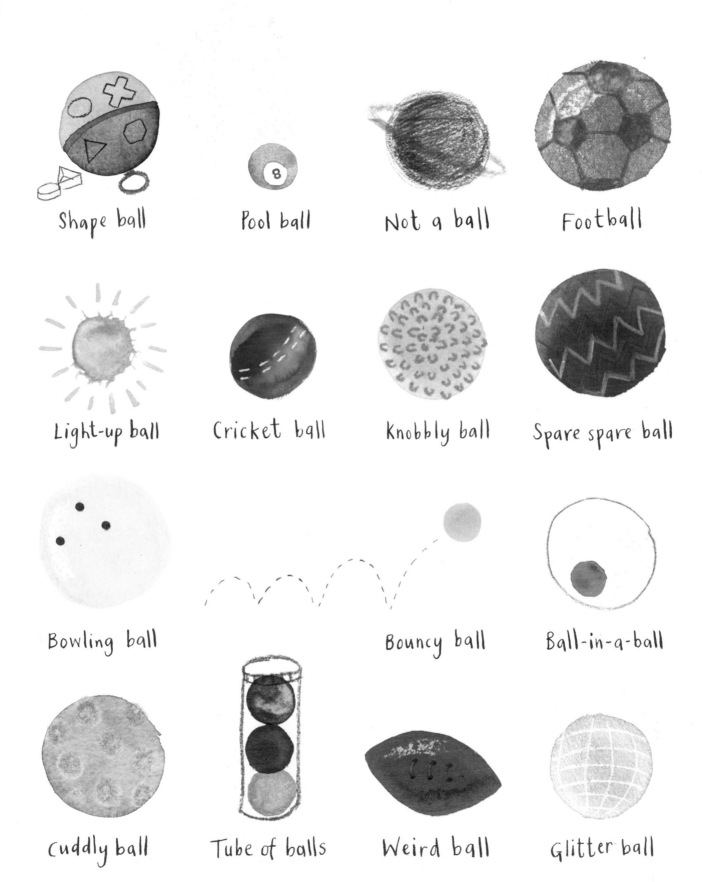

Shape ball

Pool ball

Not a ball

Football

Light-up ball

Cricket ball

Knobbly ball

Spare spare ball

Bowling ball

Bouncy ball

Ball-in-a-ball

Cuddly ball

Tube of balls

Weird ball

Glitter ball

To Leila, Edward and Seth, whose grandfather, Jim,
always gave me books for my birthday.

With special thanks to Hannah and Kerrie

First published 2019 by Macmillan Children's Books
an imprint of Pan Macmillan
20 New Wharf Road, London N1 9RR
Associated companies throughout the world
www.panmacmillan.com

ISBN 978-1-5098-5229-1 (HB)
ISBN 978-1-5098-5230-7 (PB)
ISBN 978-1-5290-0846-3 (EB)

Text and illustrations copyright © Nicola Kent 2019

The right of Nicola Kent to be identified as the author and illustrator of this work
has been asserted by her in accordance with the Copyright, Designs and Patents Act 1988.

9 8 7 6 5 4 3 2 1

A CIP catalogue record for this book
is available from the British Library.

Printed in China

Terry
and the
Brilliant
Book

Nicola Kent

MACMILLAN CHILDREN'S BOOKS

Terry and Sue were best friends.

Every birthday they gave each other a ball.
In the opinion of Terry and Sue, you can never
have too many balls.

They batted them,

they bounced them,

and they bashed them
high into the air.

Terry and Sue LOVED balls. Which is why
it was such a surprise when, for his next
birthday, Sue gave Terry . . .

Terry and Sue tried batting the book.

They tried bouncing the book.

They tried bashing the book as high as they could.

Stay there

But it didn't work very well. Sue decided to go and get Terry a ball after all.

But when she got back . . .

. . . Terry was READING the book!

And the beginning was really rather good.

Sue was glad that Terry liked the present after all,
but she was starting to feel left out.

Sue gave up and went home. She hoped that Terry
would finish the book before they went to the cinema.

When it was time to meet Sue for the film, Terry
found he was able to walk and read at the same time.

The cinema was a comfy place to read. It was just a shame that when the film was funny, the book was sad . . .

. . . and when the film was sad, the book was funny.

And it was a shame when Terry and Sue were asked to leave.

That was a bit embarrassing

Terry invited Sue for dinner to say sorry.
He found it easy to read while he cooked.

But the meal didn't turn
out quite as he'd planned.

Terry felt bad about the horrible dinner, but at least he had the brilliant book. And that night, he read it to the very end.

At the park the next morning, Terry was sad that he'd finished the book. Still, at least he had more time to play with Sue.

And they batted, bounced and bashed their ball until it got stuck in a bush.

Terry went to fetch it.

But when he came out of the bush,
Sue's head was buried in the book!

It was nice that Suc liked the book too, but soon Terry wished she'd stop reading it.

Eventually, he gave up and went home. At least Sue would have to stop when it was time for their yoga class.

But she didn't! Sue found that yoga was the perfect place to carry on with the book. Unfortunately, when they were meant to be breathing calmly, Sue got to a scary bit . . .

. . . and when they were meant to be balancing on one leg, Sue got to a silly bit.

And when they were meant to be stretching
like cats, Terry remembered his favourite bit.

Terry and Sue were asked to leave and never come back.

Terry went home.

He missed batting, bouncing and bashing balls.

He missed the brilliant book.

But most of all,
he missed Sue.

When Terry went to meet Sue the next morning,
he really hoped she'd finished the book.

And she had! Hurrah!
Now they could play ball.

It was so brilliant.
Thank you for lending
it to me

Thank you for
giving it to me

But then Sue said she'd
got some more books
from the library and
Terry's heart sank.

Uh oh

Luckily, Sue had balls in her bag too. It wasn't just Terry who missed them. And so the best friends batted, bounced and bashed balls for ages and ages.

And after that, they oohed, ahhed and ha-ha-ha-ed at books for ages and ages.

On the way home, Terry and Sue talked about how brilliant books were and how much they liked them, but how they would also never stop liking balls.

I loved that bit where...

oh yes
and that
bit when...

Ooh and it
was funny
when...

But it was a
bit scary when...

Terry and Sue are best friends.
Every birthday they give each other a ball or a book.

In their opinion, you can't go wrong with either.

CINEMA

Yoga land

Omm

READING STRICTLY PROHIBITED

LIBRARY

CLUCK

RECIPES GALORE

How to STEAK CHINESE

Best Yoga Position Ever!

BEST FILMS EVER!

You can play
ball games in
the library,
can't you?

Great big book

Little tiny book

Map book

Holey book

Broken book

Cloth book

Activity book

Notebook

Pop-up book

PARP!
Loud book

Thick book

Thin book

Fact book

Fixed book

Brand new book

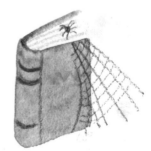
Very old book

Book without words

Book without pictures

Buggy book

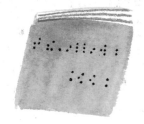

Braille book

Lost book

Found book

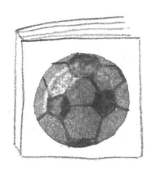

Ball book

Scary book

Film book

Flap book

Cookbook

Halfway-through book

Yoga book

Tasty book

Boring book

Brilliant book